A WOODLAND MYSTERY™

The Search for the Lost Cave

A WOODLAND MYSTERY
By Irene Schultz

To my dear friends at Allers
Boulder River Ranch

A Woodland Mystery

The Search for the Lost Cave
©1996 Story by Irene Schultz
Cover and cameo illustrations by Taylor Bruce
Interior illustrations by Merideth Yasui
Map illustration by Alicia Kramer
©1996 Wright Group Publishing, Inc.

Wright Group Development Team: Peter Beveridge, Marcie Bovetz,
Katherine Campbell, Miriam Featherston, Karen Koll, Debra Lee,
Karin Snelson, RV Stuckey, Rebel Williams

The Wright Group
19201 120th Avenue NE
Bothell, WA 98011

Printed in the United States of America

10 9 8 7 6 5 4 3 2

ISBN: 0-7802-7232-3

What family solves mysteries...has adventures all over the world...and loves oatmeal cookies?

It's the Woodlanders!

Sammy Westburg (10 years old)
His sister Kathy Westburg (13)
His brother Bill Westburg (14)
His best friend Dave Briggs (16)
His best grown-up friend Mrs. Tandy
And Mop, their little dog!

The children all lost their parents, but with Mrs. Tandy have made their own family.

Why are they called the Woodlanders? Because they live in a big house in the Bluff Lake woods. On Woodland Street!

Together they find fun, mystery, and adventure. What are they up to now?

Read on!

Meet the Woodlanders!

Sammy Westburg
Sammy is a ten-year-old wonder! He's big for his fifth-grade class, and big-mouthed, too. He has wild hair and makes awful spider faces. Even so, you can't help liking him.

Bill Westburg
Bill, fourteen, is friendly and strong, and only one inch taller than his brother Sammy. He loves Sammy, but pokes him to make him be quiet! He's in junior high.

Kathy Westburg
Kathy, thirteen, is small, shy, and smart. She wants to be a doctor some day! She loves to be with Dave, and her brothers kid her about it. She's in junior high, too.

Dave Briggs

Dave, sixteen, is tall and blond. He can't walk, so he uses a wheelchair and drives a special car. He likes coaching high-school sports, solving mysteries, and reading. And Kathy!

Mrs. Tandy

Sometimes the kids call her Mrs. T. She's Becky Tandy, their tall, thin, caring friend. She's always ready for a new adventure, and for making cookies!

Mop

Mop is the family's little tan dog. Sometimes they have to leave him behind with friends. But he'd much rather be running after Sammy.

Table of Contents

Chapter   **Page**

1 The Letter 1

2 Flying to Montana 11

3 The Strange Clue 21

4 Sherlock Holmes for Breakfast......... 31

5 The Mountain Meadow 39

6 The Wonderful Rock 49

7 Back at the Ranch............................ 57

8 The Tall Tree Rodeo........................ 65

9 Dave to the Rescue........................... 73

10 The Diary 79

11 The Weather Balloon 89

12 Detectives at Work 99

13 The Great Detective Dog................ 109

THE WOODLANDERS

IMPORTANT: OPEN AT ONCE

Chapter 1:
The Letter

Thirteen-year-old Kathy Westburg stood on the front porch, smiling from ear to ear.

She said, "Our house looks beautiful. I'm so glad to be back home!"

Her two brothers were already running up the driveway in the woods. They were each holding three suitcases. Ten-year-old Sammy shouted, "Beat you to the door, Bill!"

He jumped up the steps two at a time.

But he dropped one suitcase. It popped open. Clothes flew out onto the porch.

Bill, fourteen, scooped them up for him and closed the case.

Sixteen-year-old Dave Briggs wheeled himself up the ramp to the porch. He had a big suitcase across his wheelchair.

Mrs. Tandy followed him up.

The five Woodlanders were back in Bluff Lake!

Bill opened the door and they all hurried inside.

Their little tan dog Mop was already

home from their friend's house. He ran in circles, barking and jumping.

Bill got down on his knees to pet him.

Mop gave him a big wet lick on the chin.

Kathy set two big brown paper bags on the table.

Sammy grabbed them and dumped out the letters.

He yelled, "Look at this pile! And there are more bags of mail outside! Man, we go to England for a teeny old vacation and everybody decides to write!"

Some of the letters slid to the floor.

Bill said, "Come on, Sammy. This is your second mess in two minutes!"

Dave leaned over the side of his wheelchair. He picked up some of the letters that had dropped.

He said, "Hey, guys! Wait a minute! One of these letters is addressed to the Woodlanders. It's from my history teacher.

"You remember Mr. Adams? You met him that day he walked me home. It's marked IMPORTANT: OPEN AT ONCE."

He opened it and read it out loud.

Dear Dave and family,

I'm at my family ranch in Montana. I've been trying to reach you by phone.

You know the lost cave I keep looking for? Well, no luck this summer, either. Now it's almost time for school to start. There are only two weeks left to hunt for it. Can you join me?

We have a big cabin ready for you.

I need your help.

Call soon,

Abe Adams

Dave said, "Too bad we missed out on that! He's got less than two weeks left to find the lost cave. This letter was mailed five days ago."

Bill said, "Drag. Only nine more days to look."

Mrs. Tandy said, "And it would probably take us days to get ready to leave again. All our clothes are dirty from our trip!"

Kathy looked around at all their suitcases and groaned.

Sammy said, "And it would take a couple of days just to read our mail."

Dave said, "Still, I wish we could have gone to the ranch. Even if it WAS only for nine days. Mr. Adams told us about it in class.

"It's just a hundred miles from Billings.

"You guys could ride horseback up in the mountains. Or we could all go fishing for trout. And there are a million wildflowers everywhere."

Kathy said, "Hmm ... we helped find a lost treasure in England. Maybe we could find a lost cave in Montana."

Sammy said, "I KNOW we could!"

Suddenly Mrs. Tandy said, "Well, why DON'T we go! What's really to stop us?"

Bill said, "But what about the mail?"

Kathy said, "We can bring the rest of it inside ... to read when we get back."

Bill asked, "And the dirty clothes?"

Mrs. Tandy said, "No problem! We can dump them all out on our beds and just pull out what we need. Then we can wash them in Billings."

Kathy asked, "Perfect. But what about Mop? I hate to leave him again."

Dave said, "We can take him. But we will have keep him on a leash or in the cabin. Some bear would love him for dinner."

Sammy said, "Nothing's going to get Mop for a meal! I'll watch him."

Dave said "Well, what do you say? I'll call the airport for tickets. And call ahead to rent a car in Billings. And let Mr. Adams know!"

Suddenly everyone was running around and laughing.

They brought in the rest of the suitcases.

They brought in the rest of the mail.

They chose their clothes.

They re-packed.

They carried out their suitcases.

They put a leash on Mop.

Sammy said, "Good-bye, house!" and carried Mop out.

Dave got in behind the wheel of his hand-controlled car.

Everyone piled in.

In an hour they were at the airport.

In another hour they were on a plane to Billings, Montana.

Mop lay sleeping in a dog carrier. He didn't know he was on the way to the biggest adventure of his life.

Chapter 2:
Flying to Montana

The jet took off.

Not long after that, lunch was served.

Sammy ate everything but his cake.
He saved that on his tray to eat later.

He said, "OK, Dave. Now tell us what you know about the cave.

"How was it found?

"How was it lost?"

Dave said, "Mr. Adams told our history class this story ...

"His grandfather built the Big Rock River Ranch years ago. He raised cattle there.

"But now it's a vacation ranch.

"Anyway, Grandfather Adams built a small log cabin near the Big Rock River."

Sammy said, "Wow! A real log cabin?"

Dave nodded. "It had a dirt floor. Wind blew through the walls, and between the logs. The first winter Grandfather Adams lived there alone. He was twenty years old."

Kathy said, "That sounds pretty lonely."

Dave said, "And hard. That first

winter was really cold. Day after day he fed logs into his fireplace and never left the cabin.

"It was dark outside, and windy. And the snow was really deep.

"Grandfather Adams worked all the time.

"He made a pair of snowshoes out of wood and cowhide strips. They looked like double-sized tennis rackets with short handles.

"Then one morning he woke up to bright sunshine.

"He laced his snowshoes onto his boots. He put on his warmest clothes. Off he went, to explore for the day.

"By noon he was way up high on a mountainside. His snowshoes kept him from sinking into the soft snow.

"He was having a fine time.

"But suddenly everything went wrong."

Sammy broke in. "What? It was a bear, wasn't it!"

Kathy said, "Bears sleep all winter, Sammy."

Dave said, "Nope. Not a bear. A horrible snowstorm started blowing down along the mountains.

"The day went icy cold. Huge piles of snow began to build up.

"Grandpa Adams started down the mountain, but it was slow going.

"He was afraid he would die of cold before he got down to his cabin.

"He looked around to see if he could make a shelter.

"Then he saw a big, dark opening. It was a cave in the mountainside, right above his head."

Sammy shouted, "The lost cave!"

Bill poked him.

Dave smiled and went on. "He climbed a few feet up to the opening. He fell inside ... worn-out, but safe from the storm.

"The floor of the cave was all loose stuff. Dirt. Stones. Tiny animal bones. Dry pine needles.

15

"It was so soft he scooped out a nest to sleep in."

Bill asked, "Well, how long did the storm last?"

Dave said, "All through the afternoon and night. Mr. Adams said the next morning his grandfather opened his eyes in surprise.

"A sharp ray of sunlight had hit the wall in front of him. It was so bright it woke him up.

"There on the wall he saw some drawings in red lines. Animals, he thought.

"He looked out of the mouth of the cave. He saw treetops and the river shining in the sun.

"The storm was over!

"But he felt cold and sick.

"He strapped on his snowshoes.

"He walked all morning, down the mountain.

"At last he got to his cabin. He made a big fire. He crawled into bed.

"For months he was sick with a fever. He dreamed terrible dreams. He was out of his mind part of the time.

"He ate only dried beef and water because he was too sick to hunt.

"He could hardly lift logs onto the fire.

"But somehow he lived through it. In the spring he slowly got well. He remembered the cave, and tried to find it. But he never could.

"To this day it's still lost!

"Some people in the Big Rock River Valley call it the Ghost Cave. Some say there never was a cave. They say Grandfather Adams just imagined it.

"They say he was sick in the head from fever.

"But Mr. Adams believes it's there, above the ranch. He keeps looking for it every summer. His son and daughter used to hunt with him. Now they run the ranch, and they're too busy.

"That's why he wants our help."

Mrs. Tandy said, "What a great mystery! It's perfect for us to try to solve."

Sammy said, "TRY! TRY? We won't just TRY!"

He jumped out of his plane seat. He put his tray down on it.

He said, "We WILL find that cave! It's no ghost cave, I know it!"

He waved both his fists in the air.

People on the plane were giving him funny looks.

Bill said, "Calm down, Sammy. You know we only have nine days. Maybe we won't be able to find it that fast."

Sammy said, "You make me mad! I'll find it ALONE if I have to.

"And then you'll have to give me a dollar to see the cave drawings! THEN you'll believe the cave is real!"

Then he sat down hard ... right on top of his cake!

Chapter 3:
The Strange Clue

Just as Sammy got the cake off his pants, the plane was landing.

They went to find Mop and their bags.

They rented a van.

They drove to town.

They bought fishing licenses.

They did their laundry.

Then they piled back into the van. For an hour they passed fields and hills. They saw only four cars on the road.

All of a sudden Bill cried out, "Look over there to the right! Between those hills!"

Sammy said, "Oh my gosh! Is that a deer? What happened to its face? Looks like something stretched it."

Mrs. Tandy stopped the van on the roadside. She said, "Say, I think that's an antelope."

Kathy said, "Oh, there's another one!"

About twenty more antelopes ran out from the hills.

After a while Mrs. Tandy started the van. The antelopes began to leap high in the air.

Sammy said, "Hey! One of them jumped over his brother!"

Bill said, "I'm going to watch for them from now on."

But they didn't see any more antelopes. Instead they saw eighteen mule deer with huge ears. Then they drove into the river valley.

For thirty more bumpy miles they went along the river road.

Now there were mountains all around them. Up and up they went, past pine trees and giant rocks.

At last Sammy said, "Hey, where IS the ranch, anyway? Do you think we passed it?"

Just at that moment they saw a cowboy riding horseback on the side of the road.

Mrs. Tandy pulled the van to a stop.

Dave called out the window, "Excuse

me! Can you tell me where the Big Rock River Ranch is?"

The cowboy rode right over to the van. He reached in and grabbed Dave's shoulder.

He said, "Dave, am I glad to see you! Don't you know me with my beard? It's me, Abe Adams!

"Hello, Becky. Hi, everybody!"

He leaned in through the window and shook hands with them all. "Howdy! You're a sight for sore eyes.

"Come on! Follow me to the ranch!"

He led them around the bend in the road.

There was the ranch, to the right. The river flowed below, to the left. The road ran between the two.

Mr. Adams took them to a log cabin. It had three big bedrooms, with two beds in each room.

There was a pot-bellied iron stove in the biggest one.

There was a pile of wood and kindling to build a fire.

Mr. Adams said, "You un-pack. I'll run and tell my wife Ella and the others you're here. You'll meet them all at dinner in an hour."

When Mr. Adams came back, they were all ready.

Dave said, "We can't wait to check out the ranch. And of course, to find the cave! Could we drive around a little?"

Mr. Adams said, "You really mean it? I'm so glad. I thought you'd be too tired to start the search today."

He led his horse to the corral.

Then they all took off together in the van.

Mr. Adams said, "Becky, head back two miles north, the way you came. The ranch is long and thin. It stretches four miles along the river.

"The mountains behind it are all national park land."

Bill laughed. "Then the cave really belongs to the U.S.? That's a relief. Sammy was going to charge me a dollar to get in ... if we found it."

Sammy pointed to a big log house. He asked, "Who lives there?"

Mr. Adams said, "The park rangers. They watch for forest fires, and keep the trails clear."

Sammy said, "I think I'll be a ranger when I grow up. Look at their horses! And that jeep!"

Mr. Adams pointed to a spot along the river.

He said, "I used to find arrowheads down there when I was a boy.

"My grandpa used to say it was the workshop of the American Indians ... they threw away the arrowheads that didn't chip right."

Sammy said, "I'm going to look for some here tomorrow."

Dave said, "I sure wish I could ride horses in the mountains with you guys tomorrow. But maybe I can do some exploring with my field glasses."

Mr. Adams took his wallet out of his pocket. He pulled out a folded piece of paper.

He said, "I carry this with me all the

time, Dave. My grandfather wrote it the day he got back from the cave. But after that, he was so sick he forgot what it meant."

Sammy said, "What does it say? It's our only clue!"

Dave read the wrinkled, soft paper aloud.

There's a lion and a lamb
Across below, and here I am

Mr. Adams said, "My grandpa and our whole family searched the land below the mountain meadow.

"That's where the sheep graze, and where mountain lions live. But here I am fifty years later, still searching.

"Grandpa loved to write poems, but he must have been clean out of his mind when he wrote this one.

"He made me promise I would find the cave someday. He said he'd never rest easy in his grave until then."

Sammy said, "Oh, no! Do you mean your grandfather's ghost is wandering around the mountains?"

Kathy laughed. "Come on, Sammy! That's not what he means! But just to be safe, I'm staying with you, tomorrow, Dave."

Then she blushed bright pink.

Mr. Adams said, "Good idea! Then you two can plan the search from down here. And study that poem."

Bill said, "Since it's the only clue, somebody better figure it out!"

But Dave was thinking.

He leaned over to Kathy and whispered, "I think we might already have another clue. But I don't want to tell anyone about it until I'm sure."

29

Chapter 4:
Sherlock Holmes for
Breakfast

At 6:00 the next morning everyone woke up to a loud CLANG!

Bill ran into the big room where Dave and Sammy slept.

There was Sammy with a silly grin on his face. He said, "I made a fire in the stove for a surprise. I guess I dropped the lid back on a little hard."

Mrs. Tandy and Kathy came in. Mrs. Tandy asked, "What was that? It sounded like a Chinese gong."

Sammy said, "Aw, I was just trying to warm up the cabin for when you got up later. Now I bet you're all mad at me."

Bill said, "We had to get up anyway, Sammy. We went to bed at eight last night. We've had ten hours of sleep already."

Kathy said, "Breakfast isn't until eight o'clock. If we hurry we can take a look at the arrowhead place first."

In twenty-five minutes they were on the gravel beach at the river's edge. Dave lowered himself out of his chair to look at the stones.

Kathy and Sammy were fishing with rubber worms. They walked along the gravel in their sneakers.

Kathy said, "I'm going to walk a little into the water to fish. I want to see how cold it is. YIKES! It's freezing!"

She hurried back out.

Sammy trotted a little deeper into the water. He waved to make sure Kathy was looking at him.

The stones were round and slippery. Rushing water flowed between them and his smooth rubber soles.

He held tight to his fishing pole but his feet flew out from under him.

The next minute Sammy was sitting in ice cold water.

Mrs. Tandy shouted, "My lands!"

She and Bill rushed over to Sammy. They helped him stand up. They tried to lead him out.

Sammy said, "No, no! Leave me alone. Don't pull my arm!"

Bill cried, "What's wrong, Sammy? Did you hurt your arm?"

Sammy shouted, "I'm OK! But something is pulling my line. I've got a fish!"

He began to reel in his line.

Everyone started yelling.

Dave called, "Reel in fast!"

34

Mrs. Tandy shouted, "Keep your line tight!"

Kathy said, "Don't keep the tip of the pole so low!"

Sammy yelled, "I think it's a big one! I think it's a giant one!"

He got so excited, he yanked the fish right out of the water.

It flew through the air.

It landed on the gravel bed right in front of where Dave was sitting.

Sammy ran over to his fish. "It's not so big after all. It's only about as long as my shoe."

Bill joked, "Any fish the size of your shoe is plenty big."

Dave said, "And it's the first fish caught today. You win the first-fish prize. One dollar."

Sammy picked up his fish to take the hook out.

Kathy looked down at the wet stones where the fish had landed.

She cried, "Look at that!"

She reached for something wet and shiny. She held it up for everyone to see.

In her hand lay a beautiful gray arrowhead.

They all crowded around.

Mrs. Tandy gasped.

Kathy said, "Look, the back end is a little broken, but the point end is perfect. And Sammy's fish found it!"

Dave said, "This gravel bed must really have been an arrowhead workshop! Grandpa Adams was right!"

Then Sammy took the hook out of his fish. It was still alive and flapping.

He kissed it on the top of its cold, wet head. Carefully he put it back into the river.

The fish lay still on the bottom for a moment. Then it shook its tail and was gone.

Dave called after it, "Thanks, old fish."

Bill said, "Your fish wasn't big, Sammy, but it was a great detective."

Sammy said, "I know. That's why I didn't keep him. It would be like eating Sherlock Holmes for breakfast."

Chapter 5:
The Mountain Meadow

They hurried back to the ranch in the van.

They found Mr. Adams and told him about Sammy's fish and the arrowhead.

Just then they heard the low gong of the big iron ranch bell.

Mr. Adams said, "Time for breakfast!"

The other ranch guests around the table were excited about the arrowhead.

One woman said, "I've been here on vacation for two weeks. I didn't even think to look for arrowheads!

"But I'm coming back NEXT year, and finding one!"

They had pancakes and ham and eggs for breakfast. There was home-made bread, still warm, with wild berry jam.

Sammy finally said, "I'm ready for our mountain ride. But you'll have to lift me onto the horse. I'm too stuffed to move."

Mr. Adams said, "Don't worry. I'll help you up. I'd help a tiger onto a horse if he'd help me find this cave."

They went down to the corral.

The ranch helpers had the horses saddled.

Mrs. Tandy mounted first, on Old Joe. She got her left foot into the left stirrup. She swung her right leg over the horse. It was easy for her, because her legs were so long.

Bill and Sammy had a little more trouble. Their horses were both big, so the stirrups were high off the ground.

Bill found a log for them to stand on. Then they got up easily on Big Boy and Suzy.

They waved good-bye to Kathy and Dave.

In a line, they followed Mr. Adams on Buckshot. He led them through the rangers' yard.

Dusty, the family's collie, followed behind the horses.

Mr. Adams turned and said, "I'm going to take you up a trail that zig-zags back and forth. It covers the two mountains right behind the ranch."

Sammy asked, "How far up will we go?"

Mr. Adams said, "The ranch is right at five thousand feet. We can ride to eight thousand feet, into the high meadows.

"Remember the poem ...'There's a lion and a lamb. Across, below, and here I am.'

"I'll show you mountain-lion country where the sheep some times feed. Maybe you can find some clue we've missed all these years."

The mountain trail was only about two feet wide. It led them through bushes and over rocks.

Sometimes they rode along the edges of cliffs.

Sammy said, "Holy cats! That's a hundred feet straight down! I'm never looking over the side of the trail again!"

Just then his horse looked down the mountain. She took a step to the very edge.

Sammy yelled, "Whoa! Stop, you crazy horse!"

Mr. Adams called back, "Keep her reins tight. Suzy's a smart little pig. She will grab anything she can, if you don't hold her head up."

For a while they rode in bright sunshine.

They passed through cool forests.

After an hour they stopped at a spring

gushing from some rocks.

They led their horses to the water, one by one.

Mr. Adams said, "We should rest for a while. The air is thinner in the mountains. If you're not used to it, you get tired fast."

Bright flowers grew around them. Bunches of purple. Clumps of white. Big yellow flowers with brown fuzzy centers.

Mrs. Tandy said, "My, they look good enough to eat!"

Mr. Adams smiled and said, "Well, then, Becky, we'd better move along before you DO eat one.

"Those deep purple ones are larkspur. Those over there are locoweed. They make horses get sick and crazy. I don't know what they'd do to a pretty woman!"

Sammy poked Bill. He whispered,

"Looks like Mrs. T. might have a new boyfriend!"

Bill whispered, "Don't be stupid. Mr. Adams is married, remember?"

They got on the horses again and rode for another hour.

The trail led them over a rise of land ... and suddenly they all pulled their horses to a stop. What a sight!

A beautiful wild meadow full of flowers stretched out in front of them. All around rose the mountaintops.

As they looked around, Bill saw two big black spots on the mountainside a little way above them.

He shouted, "If those aren't caves, what are they!"

Mr. Adams laughed. "Those ARE caves. We've climbed up into both of them. But neither one of them is THE cave."

Sammy said, "Besides, they're too high. The poem said to look across and BELOW the lion and the lamb. That must mean across and below the meadow."

Mrs. Tandy asked, "Are there other mountain fields where sheep graze around here?"

Mr. Adams said, "Nope. None near enough that Grandpa Adams could have reached them by snowshoe in half a day."

They rode for an hour on the mountain right below the field.

They got off their horses and looked in back of the bushes and rocks.

At last they stopped for lunch.

46

In their saddlebags were sandwiches, oranges, and cookies.

Bill said, "Well, there are just too many trees, and too many bushes, and too many rocks, and too many places you can't get to."

Sammy took a big bite out of his sandwich.

He said, mouth full, "I think we should report back to Kathy and Dave. We've got to make some kind of plan or we might run out of time."

Mr. Adams said, "You're right."

Bill said, "You know, I think I can imagine how much the Native Americans loved this land.

"They hunted in this field, and fished in the river below.

"They had their arrowhead workshop. I wonder if they knew about that cave and the drawings. Maybe they did, and thought it was a magic place."

Mrs. Tandy asked, "Why do you say that, Bill?"

Bill said, "Dave once told me about a cave in France where people had painted animals on the walls. Thousands of years ago.

"They used the cave to help the tribe remember their stories and history."

Mr. Adams said, "You're right, Bill. In fact, I'm probably the one who told Dave about that cave in France."

Sammy said, "When we start back, let's keep our eyes open for the cave all the way down."

Mrs. Tandy said, "I hate to leave this place."

Bill said, "Me, too. I'm sure sorry Dave and Kathy weren't here. They missed out on all the fun."

Chapter 6:
The Wonderful Rock

But at that very moment, Kathy, Dave, and Mop were riding north. They were going toward the arrowhead place.

Ed, the ranch caretaker, was driving them.

Dave pointed to a little grassy field right above the gravel bed.

He said, "There's the spot to eat our lunch. Ed, can we drive down to it?"

He said, "No problem. I'll check in on you every hour or so. Then I'll pick you up as soon as I see the others coming back from their ride, OK?"

Kathy said, "You bet! See you later!"

She helped Dave into his wheelchair, then tied Mop to a tree.

She sat on a rock near Dave. Then she asked, "Why did you want to come here again?"

Dave said, "Well, I just keep thinking about the arrowheads. They're the only real sign of human life around here."

Kathy said, "So you think the arrowheads could help us find the cave?"

Dave said, "Well, maybe. That's what I wanted to tell you earlier. That the cave was important to whoever painted it.

"And the arrowheads were important to the Native Americans.

"So it makes sense that the cave might be above us. Near the arrowhead place."

Kathy said, "But what if the drawings were done by people hundreds of years before the Native Americans?"

Dave said, "Well, even if that's true, I bet those later tribes still would have thought the cave was holy in some way."

Kathy nodded. "So maybe even then they would want to spend time near it."

Dave said, "Yep. I think that cave could be straight above us."

He pointed at the mountain. He didn't know that just a little way around the same mountain were the two caves Bill had seen.

All that Kathy and Dave could see

was their side of the mountain, covered by a blanket of trees.

Dave let himself down from his chair to the grass.

Kathy put their two lunch bags on top of a red raincoat.

She said, "This is the best lunch spot ever. Look at the river rushing along. And listen to it. And smell that pine smell."

The two young people sat against a tree, eating. Their oranges tasted sweet and warm and juicy.

Butterflies danced around them.

Bees hummed in and out of flowers.

The wind blew softly.

After they had eaten, Kathy tied Mop closer to where they were sitting.

Dave looked around him. He said, "This has to be the most beautiful place in the world. Even the rocks are pretty."

Most of the rocks were round, or almost round. There was one near Dave that was about the size of a volleyball ... but flat on top.

The rock was tipped up out of the ground. Lumps of fresh dirt lay next to it.

Mop sniffed it.

He began to shake all over.

He barked at the rock.

Then he jumped away from it.

Dave said, "I bet a bear lifted that rock up, looking for insects to eat. Mop must smell him."

He reached over to the rock and turned it all the way over.

For a moment Kathy and Dave just stared.

They couldn't say a word.

Their hearts were jumping like frogs.

At last Kathy said, "Dave, that's not a rock. That's a bowl."

Dave said, "Kathy, I can't believe it! It IS a bowl. A solid stone bowl."

He pulled it closer to him.

The sides of the bowl were about as thick as his little finger.

They were all smooth, inside and out.

Kathy said, "I've never seen anything like it."

Dave said, "I wonder who made it? Someone spent months grinding out the inside. Finding this is the greatest thing Mop's ever done.

"And I don't know why, but it makes

me feel even more like the cave is near here!"

He and Kathy passed the bowl back and forth between them.

Then Dave hugged it to his chest.

He said, "It's wonderful. I'm only sorry about one thing."

Kathy asked, "What's that?"

Dave said, "It's too bad the others weren't here. They missed out on all the fun."

55

Chapter 7:
Back at the Ranch

The others rode down from the mountains.

Kathy and Dave were waiting in the rangers' yard.

Ed sat in the van, ready to drive them back to the ranch.

Kathy and Dave were shouting and waving at the horseback riders.

One of the rangers was with them. He was waving, too.

Mr. Adams called, "Hi, Tyler! Dave? Kathy? What's all the shouting about?"

Sammy rode up and said, "We've GOT to think of a way to get you into the mountain field, Dave. You, too, Kathy. There's SO much to see up there."

Dave said, "There's a lot to see down here, too, Sammy. LOOK!"

He held up the stone bowl. Everyone shouted at once.

"How beautiful!"

"My gosh!"

"Wow!"

"Where did you get THAT?"

Mr. Adams took hold of the bowl.

"Where did you find THIS?"

Dave and Kathy told him all about their picnic, and Mop's barking.

Bill said, "That Mop is a great detective dog. I'd get off my horse and hug him, but I'm not sure I could get back on."

Mop wagged his tail, and Dusty barked.

Mr. Adams laughed. "We all are tired from the ride. Let's get back to the ranch and look at the bowl there."

Kathy asked, "Did you find any clues on your ride?"

Bill said, "Sure. I found some caves, two caves. But neither one was the lost cave."

Dave asked, "Where were they?"

Mrs. Tandy said, "Right around North Mountain."

She pointed to the mountain above the arrowhead place.

The ranger said, "Say, Dave, if you want to go up to the mountain meadow Monday, let me know. I check it out every once in a while with my jeep.

"I go around to the old miners' road."

Dave said, "Thanks, Tyler. Maybe I'll take you up on that."

Back at the ranch the riders went to the corral.

Sammy said, "Boy, I never knew I was such a good rider! But ... one thing. How do I get off?"

Mr. Adams said, "Watch me. You hold your reins in your left hand against the saddle horn.

"You stand up in your left stirrup and swing your right leg next to your left.

"Then you lift yourself up a little with both hands on the saddle. Then you slide down on BOTH FEET."

Sammy said, "Here's how you do it! Just watch me, everybody."

He followed Mr. Adams's directions. But when he slid down to the ground his knees caved in. He landed flat on his bottom, HARD.

He cried out, "Hey! What happened to my knees? They turned into noodles!"

Mr. Adams laughed. "Sometimes when you've been riding for hours, Sammy, that happens."

Bill got off his horse. He lifted Sammy up.

Sammy said, "Thanks, Bill," and then hit him. "That's so you know how much that hurt."

Then they all climbed into the van for the short ride to the cabins.

Mr. Adams said, "I'm taking you and all the guests to see some great riding tomorrow.

"The cave hunt will have to wait until Sunday. My son and his wife won't be around tomorrow. That leaves Ella and me to take care of all the guests!"

Bill asked, "Where are we all going?"

Mr. Adams answered, "To the town of Tall Tree. It's forty miles from here. They're having a rodeo."

Sammy shouted, "Yipee!"

Then Bill said, "Well, so far we've found an arrow head and a bowl, and two wrong caves. Not bad for one day.

"I wonder what's waiting for us at the rodeo tomorrow?" he said with a laugh.

Chapter 8:
The Tall Tree Rodeo

At 10:00 the next morning a parade of cars bumped down the river road.

Mr. Adams drove six guests in a car he used only on special days.

It was a purple 1945 Packard. Its metal trim shone in the sun.

Mrs. Tandy drove the Woodlanders in the van.

Ed drove all the ranch hands in a pick-up truck.

A station wagon and the rangers' jeep came last.

In an hour they reached Tall Tree.

The town was filled with people.

Bill exclaimed, "It's like an anthill here!"

Sammy asked, "Are we going to stop here for lunch? I'm hungry already."

Kathy said, "They're selling hot dogs and chips at the rodeo grounds. Let's eat there."

They did. Big fat hot dogs. Big juicy hamburgers. Orange soda.

While they were finishing their lunch, a woman came over to them. She looked very worried.

She said, "I wonder if you could help me? I just dropped off my husband and his friends. Now I have a flat tire, and no one to fix it."

Dave said, "Don't worry. My friends and I have changed tires lots of times."

Sammy said, "And we never get TIRED of it, either!"

Everybody groaned a little.

But in fifteen minutes they had the spare tire on the car. The woman offered to pay them, but the Woodlanders wouldn't take any money.

The woman said, "I can't thank you enough. I just hope I can help YOU out sometime."

Then she drove off to park her car.

They all walked through the grassy field next to the rodeo grounds.

There were hundreds of horse trailers parked there.

Men and women and boys and girls were washing and brushing their horses.

Mrs. Tandy said, "Well, I don't know why, but I love the smell of this rodeo. Hot dogs and horses and hay and coffee. It's not perfume, but it's very good."

Soon they came to the rodeo bleachers.

They pulled Dave up a couple of rows in his chair.

Bill said, "Wow! Look at that!"

Ten men in Scottish kilts were standing three rows back from the Woodlanders. They had bagpipes.

Sammy called to them, "Hey, you're wearing skirts! Like some soldiers we saw in England. Do you play those bagpipes?"

One of the men said, "Sure. Our families came from Scotland long ago and settled around here.

"We keep the old customs going. We play our pipes when ever we get a chance. Haven't you heard us before?"

Dave said, "This is our first time in Montana. Abe Adams invited us up to his ranch. I'm Dave Briggs and these are my friends."

The man said, "I'm Sandy McDuff. It's funny you should mention the Adams ranch. My wife's great-grandfather used to have a cabin in back of it.

"His name was Tom Burns. It was high up on South Mountain. Right near a stream.

"We found his diary just this year in an old trunk on our ranch. Some of it's good reading, but we never did finish it. The ink's all faded and it's hard to read.

"Great-grandpa Burns was quite a man.

"He used to pan for gold in a mountain stream up there every summer.

"Got enough gold dust out to buy a piece of ranch land. Took him fifteen years, but he did it."

Dave said, "Wow! We would love to read that diary. Hey, guys! Something in it could help us find the cave!"

Bill said, "A man who lived in those mountains for fifteen years might have found that cave himself!"

Mr. McDuff said, "A cave, eh? Sorry, lads. That book means so much to my wife, I don't think she would let it out of her sight."

He looked past them. "Here she comes now."

He called, "Molly, what took you so long? I want you to meet some folks here. They're staying at the Adams place.

"I was telling them about your great-grandfather's diary. I don't suppose you would want to lend it to strangers, would you?"

Up walked Molly McDuff.

The Woodlanders could hardly believe their eyes!

She was the woman they had helped with the flat tire.

She took a good, slow look around. She said, "Well, as a matter of fact, I would, Sandy. They're about the only strangers I WOULD lend it to.

"I know them already. They came to my rescue just a while ago. They changed a flat tire for me. I'd love a way to pay them back.

"After the rodeo, we can all drive over to our ranch and get the diary for them to borrow."

Chapter 9:
Dave to the Rescue

A loudspeaker blared out, "Ladies and gentlemen! Welcome to the Tall Tree Rodeo!"

Everyone stood up. Two riders carrying

United States' flags rode into the ring. Their silver-trimmed saddles flashed in the sunlight.

They galloped around the circle. They faced the audience, while their horses trotted sideways.

Everyone sang "The Star Spangled Banner."

Then the loudspeaker announced the names of the riders. They galloped their horses around the ring.

Now the real rodeo began.

First came the wild horses. Every time a rider got onto a wild horse, it began to buck. It jumped into the air. It rounded its back. Then it landed on all four hooves. THUD!

The rider who stayed on for the wildest ride won.

Sometimes the riders were bucked off. Then two cowboys dressed like clowns would chase the wild horses away from them.

Sammy said, "Hey! Those clowns are great! I could do that. Maybe I'll be a rodeo clown when I grow up."

At last it was time for the bull riding.

A wild bull raced into the ring. The rider on his back was slipping and sliding, trying to stay on.

In a few seconds he fell off. He was hurt. The bull began to rush toward him. The animal held its head low, aiming its horns at the fallen rider.

Suddenly the two clowns ran toward the bull.

They waved bright rags to get him to run after them instead.

The rider limped out of the ring.
The clowns ran.

But one of the clowns fell down.

The bull raced toward him.

Everyone screamed. The bull could kill him!

All of a sudden, Dave ripped the cowboy hat off his head. He threw it. It sailed through the air and flew past the bull's face.

The bull turned away from the clown. It went running after Dave's hat instead.

The clown jumped up and ran out of the ring. He was saved.

Everyone was standing and cheering for Dave.

76

The bull was in a rage. He jumped and stamped on Dave's hat until it was as flat as a pancake.

Finally some cowboys on horseback drove the bull out, jumping and twisting.

The bagpipe band stood up and played Dave a song.

Sandy McDuff took off his own Scottish hat and placed it on Dave's head.

He said, "Keep this, my lad. I'll get another. It will remind you of this day when your quick wits saved a man's life!"

Kathy said shyly, "You were great, Dave."

77

Sammy said, "You were! But to tell the truth, I'd have acted just like that bull if some one tried to ride me.

"Rodeos are weird. They sure are exciting, but they seem so mean. I loved the rodeo, but I hated it, too."

Bill said, "And we know what part you loved. The hot dogs!"

TOM BURNS.
HIS BOOK.

Chapter 10:
The Diary

After the rodeo they found Mr. Adams
and told him about the diary.

Bill said, "As soon as we get it we
can head back to the ranch. We won't

even open it until you're there."

Mr. Adams said, "Sounds wonderful. I'll see you guys later then!"

Mrs. Tandy followed the McDuffs in the van.

At her ranch, Molly McDuff gave them the book.

Kathy opened the thin, old, black leather diary. Inside was written, "Tom Burns. His Book."

She said, "We will take good care of this, Mrs. McDuff. It's so nice of you to lend it to us."

She wrapped it carefully in her sweater.

Then off they drove to the Adams ranch.

But it took them longer than they expected to get back.

Just five miles before the ranch, Mrs. Tandy had to stop the van.

Running up the road toward them was a river ... a great river of sheep!

There were hundreds of sheep, walking slowly along.

B-a-a-a-h. B-a-a-a-h. They bleated to each other and munched on the grass at the roadside.

Sammy hopped out of the van with his camera. But every time he walked toward a sheep, it trotted away.

Finally they saw the end of the herd.

A big dog was running in back of it, keeping the sheep together.

At last the Woodlanders got to the ranch.

Back in the big cabin with Mr. and Mrs. Adams, they asked Kathy to begin reading the diary.

She started to read.

"It's lonely up here on my mountainside. I got this book so I'd have something that's fun to do by candlelight.

"Had good luck panning for gold today. Besides the little grains like sand, I got one the size of a pea.

"This stream is washing it down from some place in the earth above. Wish I knew where.

"I dip up a pan full of rock from the river bed. I roll the gravel and water out. There at the bottom are the heavy grains of gold sand. I dream of finding the mother-lode.

"And now to bed."

Kathy said, "His writing is so small! And it's really faded after all these years."

Dave said, "Here, Kathy, I'll read for a while."

He picked up the book and said, "He sure DID write small. I guess he was

afraid he'd run out of paper before he came down from the mountain."

On and on they read, taking turns. Mr. Adams brought sandwiches and fruit to the cabin for dinner.

They kept reading.

Mop ate a left-over sandwich and half an apple. He fell asleep on Sammy's lap.

It was 11:00 at night, and everyone was yawning. But no one wanted to stop reading the diary.

Tom Burns wrote about raccoons and deer, elk and beaver, birds and antelopes.

He told about the shapes of the mountains and the changes in the riverbed below.

Line after faint line gave them a picture of his life.

They were nearly at the end of the diary. Now it was Bill's turn to read again.

He looked at the last few pages before he began to read out loud.

He cried, "Holy cats! Listen to this!"

He started reading.

"Today was a strange one. It began in the middle of the morning, while I was panning for gold at my stream. I had a feeling some one was near me, watching me.

"I looked up and saw an old man, a Crow Indian, I think. He looked thin and tired. I stood and said, 'Welcome!' He said, 'Thank you, friend.'

"He started to walk toward me. Then he fell. I ran to him and caught him in my arms.

"I pulled him into my cabin and put him down on my bed.

"I gave him some cold stream water to drink.

"I made hot coffee and cut some bread and spread it with wild berry jelly.

"Finally he ate a little and sat up.

"His voice was faint but he wanted to talk.

"He said he had lived in these very mountains as a child.

"Now he was dying, and he wanted to die in a place that was holy to his tribe. He had walked hundreds of miles.

"'Where do you want to go?' I asked him.

"'Here,' he said. 'I have come back here.'

"He told me my cabin was on a holy spot.

"He said there is a cave straight across from here on North Mountain. 'Lower than its brothers and closer to the river.'

"He said it has strange pictures in it. No one in his tribe knew what they meant. Or who painted them.

"I asked him why, then, my place was holy. He said it was because of the rocks on the mountain cliff above my cabin.

"On the shortest day of the year the shadows hit them a special way.

"From the cave the rocks look like a lion and a lamb. And on that day, light shines full onto the drawings in the cave."

Everyone shouted, "LION and LAMB!"

Sammy cried, "Holy hot dogs!"

Mr. Adams exclaimed, "They must be the same lion and lamb from my grandpa's poem ... 'There's a lion and a lamb. Across, below, and here I am.'"

Dave said, "So it's not across and below the mountain lion meadow! It's across from and below those rocks!"

Bill said, "There must be a third cave, around the mountain from the two we saw. Hidden by trees."

Dave said, "I knew we'd find it on North Mountain!"

Kathy said, "What else does it say, Bill?"

Bill read on.

"The old man lived through the afternoon. He told me tales of his tribe. I hoped he would live if I took care of him. But he died tonight.

"Tomorrow I'll bury him in back of my cabin, below his holy rocks."

Bill said, "That's the last page. The end of the diary."

He put the book down.

Mrs. Tandy said, "My word! I feel like Molly McDuff's great-grandpa is talking to us!"

Kathy said, "And now we know there really is a cave somewhere."

Dave said, "And we will find it! I know we will! Maybe even tomorrow."

Sammy said, "I used to think teachers were mean when they made me do homework.

"But boy, am I glad they taught us all how to read. Even my stupid brother Bill!"

And he picked up poor sleepy Mop and danced with him around the cabin.

Chapter 11:
The Weather Balloon

At 6:00 the next morning, they all piled into the van. They drove to the ranger station.

They told Tyler what they knew.

Tyler said, "What a great discovery that cave would be! What can I do to help?"

Mr. Adams asked, "Do you have any idea of where the old Burns cabin was?"

Tyler said, "Why, sure, Abe. Look right here."

He lifted the bottom of a big map on the wall. He showed them another map under it.

He said, "This second map has all the old cabins and mines marked on it.

"Here it is, near the old mine road."

Dave said, "Can you get me to the place? The others are all riding up on North Mountain to look for the cave today.

"They need to be able to see where the Burns cabin was. Then they have to look across from it, and below it."

Tyler said, "It will take about three

hours in the jeep, but I can get you there."

Dave said, "We need something to show them where the cabin is, right through the trees. Can you think of how to do it?"

Tyler thought for a minute. He said, "I know what we can use. A weather balloon. Back in a few minutes!"

He left the room. When he came back he had some bags and boxes.

He said, "Let's go, Dave. Abe, we should be all set up in four hours ... by about ten o'clock. Look for the balloon then."

He handed the two-way radio to Abe. He said, "Call us to let us know what you're doing."

Then Dave got himself into the jeep. Sammy put the wheelchair in the back.

Tyler called to Abe, "Take field glasses

with you. You'll need to see where the balloon rope comes out of the treetops.

"Figure the cliff you're looking for must be right about there.

"Start out about two hours from now. We should both get to the mountains at the same time."

Tyler and Dave drove off in the jeep, down the river road. They came to a bumpy gravel road that led around back of the mountains.

The road was made of dirt and stones.

The jeep bounced around like a rubber ball.

Dave had to hold on to the window frame and the dashboard to stay up-right.

They drove up and up, hour after hour.

After a while, Dave said, "Hey! Where did the road go?"

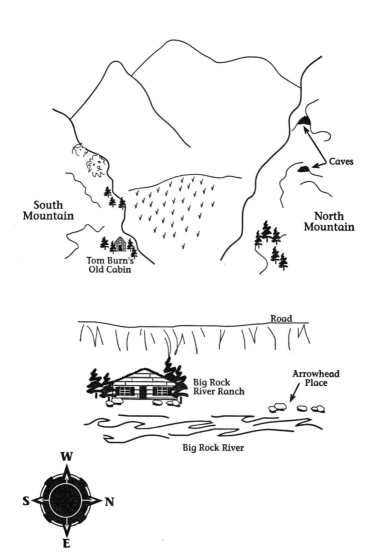

Caves

South
Mountain

North
Mountain

Tom Burn's
Old Cabin

Road

Big Rock
River Ranch

Arrowhead
Place

Big Rock River

W

S
N

E

93

They were at the edge of a beautiful meadow that spread for miles in front of them.

Tyler said, "This is the back end of the mountain meadow your friends rode over yesterday.

"We can drive through the grass over to South Mountain. Then the mine road starts up again."

Dave said, "This grassy part is worse than the road!"

They would go smoothly for a few feet and then BANG! A tire would hit a prairie-dog hole or a dry streambed. The whole jeep would tip down and then up, like a rocking chair.

At last they reached the mine road. After a while, Tyler stopped the jeep.

He brought Dave's chair to the car door and Dave got out.

Then he piled boxes and bags on

Dave's lap.

He said, "I'll pull your chair backward over to the cabin site. You just hang on to those bundles."

At last they stopped.

Tyler said, "See this?"

He pointed to a pile of stones. "This is where the old chimney was. It's all that's left of the old Burns cabin now.

"But I never did figure out what that ring of stones was, in back of the cabin site."

Dave looked toward it. He said, softly, "I think I know what it is. It must be the grave of Great-grandpa Burns's Crow Indian friend."

The two young men stared across at the mountain to the north.

Dave said, "I can't see anything that looks like a third cave. It must be hidden by those treetops against that

steep wall."

Tyler said, "Well, let's get our marker set up."

He took a shiny tank out of a box. It said HELIUM on the side.

From a bag he took a big folded piece of cloth.

He opened it.

Dave saw it was a giant cloth balloon.

Tyler tied it to a tree trunk. "I used a hundred-fifty-foot nylon rope. It's good and strong. These mountain winds can surprise you if you're not careful."

He took out a white rag. He tore it into strips.

Tyler said, "Tie these every ten feet down the rope from the balloon, like a kite tail. That way they can see the rope more easily above the treetops."

Dave said, "And they'll know where we are, even if the wind moves the balloon."

At last Tyler screwed the tank to the balloon.

He said, "Hold the rope, Dave, until the balloon is filled."

In a few minutes the balloon was about twice as big as the jeep.

Tyler un-screwed the tank. Then they let the big balloon rise slowly into the air, until it pulled at its rope.

Tyler said, "All ready. Now all we have to do is eat lunch and wait to hear from the cave hunters."

Chapter 12:
Detectives at Work

While Dave and Tyler were busy with the balloon, the rest were getting ready to ride.

At 9:00 Mr. Adams locked Dusty in

the ranch house.

He said, "This might be too hard a day, even for Dusty."

They all got on their horses.

Mr. Adams led the cave hunters to the trail behind the ranger station. They rode along it for half an hour as it zig-zagged up.

Sammy's horse was last. Sammy had hung way back from the rest ever since they left the ranch.

Mr. Adams stopped his horse. "I want you to see the ranch from here."

They looked down over the cliff.

Beneath them the trees stretched a thousand feet to the ranch.

The buildings looked like a toy town, set in a green painted field.

The river ran in a silver string below the tiny road.

The only sounds were the wind

blowing through the leaves, and the horses breathing.

Then ... barking!

Suzy, Sammy's horse, stamped her hooves at the sound.

Bill said, "Good grief. Is that Dusty? No! That sounds like Mop!"

Kathy said, "It can't be Mop. I shut him in the bedroom in the cabin."

"Yip!"

The sound seemed to be coming from the end of the line of horses.

All the riders turned their heads to look.

Sammy had a silly smile on his face.

His jacket was shaking up and down.

Bill moaned, "Saaammy ... now I know why you were riding so far behind us. And THAT'S what you were carrying inside your jacket! Mop!"

Mrs. Tandy said, "Sammy, I asked you what you had stuffed in there. You said it was something for cave hunting!"

Sammy said, "It is. My cave-hunting thing is Mop."

Kathy groaned, "Sammy, what the heck made you think he'd stay still until we got off our horses?"

Sammy said, "I gave him one of the pills the vet gave us to make him sleepy when he's on the plane. But it doesn't seem to be working."

Mop barked again.

Mr. Adams laughed. "Well, we won't turn back.

"Just zip your jacket down a little, so Mop can get more air. I've carried lots of lambs off the mountainside, just like that.

"If Mop can stand it, we can. Who knows, he may be of some help."

Forty minutes later they came to a clearing.

Bill shouted, "Look!"

To their left, on South Mountain, they saw the weather balloon.

Mrs. Tandy said, "We must be at just about the right spot."

Mr. Adams said, "That's right. The cave must be near us, maybe in that rough cliff in back of these trees.

"Let's tie our horses and walk over to the base of it."

Sammy led Mop on a long rope.

They reached the bottom of the cliff and looked upward along it.

No cave.

They pushed their way along the cliff's base through the bushes, and kept looking up.

Still no cave.

Bill said, "Do you think it's ABOVE the top edge of this cliff? Maybe that's why we can't see it."

Kathy said, "If it's that high up how could Grandpa Adams have gotten into it?"

Sammy said, "Kathy's right. That cliff's as high as a house."

Mr. Adams said, "Let's check in with Tyler and Dave now. They'll be wondering where we are."

He picked up the two-way radio from his belt and said, "U.S. Ranger Tyler? Can you hear me?"

Tyler's voice came on right away. "We hear you, but can't see you. Where are you?"

Mr. Adams said, "Right across from you. We've looked all over the face of a twenty-foot-high cliff behind the trees. We don't see a thing."

Tyler said, "Could the cave be above the cliff?"

Mr. Adams said, "That's what we wondered. But that would place it too high for Grandpa Adams's story. "Remember? He said the cave was right near his head."

Then they heard Dave's voice on the radio. "Hello? I've got an idea. What's the record snow fall around here?

"Is it possible that there could have been so much piled up that it reached to the top of that cliff?"

Mr. Adams shouted, "By golly, Dave!

That's it! Once in a while we do get a HUGE snowfall.

"My grandpa could have been on snowshoes twenty feet above where we are now. That's where he saw the cave!"

Mrs. Tandy said, "Well, we have to figure out a way to get up this cliff."

Kathy said, "What if there IS no way up?"

Bill said, "There has to be. The people who used the cave wouldn't wait for twenty feet of snow to be able to get into it."

Sammy said, "It must be up there, right above us. And we have to find it. But what do we do next?"

Bill said, "We've got to find some way to climb this cliff. It's steep, but it's rough. Maybe we can find some footholds up."

Sammy said, "That's it! I knew Mop could help us! Where's our lunch? I need it, right now!"

Chapter 13:
The Great Detective Dog

Mr. Adams said, "Lunch is in that bag over there, Sammy."

Bill said, "Sammy, how can you be thinking about food NOW?"

Sammy said, "It's always a good time to think about food. But I'm not going to eat it. I need it for Mop, the great hunter. He's a cairn terrier, you know."

Kathy said, "That's right! Cairn terriers were raised to hunt on rocks."

Dave said, "In fact, the word CAIRN means a pile of rocks."

Bill said, "But Mop's never climbed on rocks in his life! He's not even very good at climbing the steps at home."

Sammy said, "That's OK. I have a plan. Here's a tuna salad sandwich. It's perfect. It has a nice fishy smell. I bet Mop can sniff this twenty feet away."

He broke off a corner of one sandwich and fed it to Mop.

Then he broke off a couple of other corners.

He threw them onto the rocks that stuck out from the cliff wall.

He ordered, "Go fetch, Moppy!" Mop began to hop around on his hind legs and bark. He tried to scramble up the wall, but couldn't.

He ran to another spot and tried.

Then he raced back to Sammy.

Sammy pointed to the cliff wall with the rest of the tuna salad sandwich. "Go fetch, Mop."

Mop jumped straight up in the air. He grabbed the rest of the sandwich from Sammy's hand.

He ran to the end of his long rope. Then he sat down and began to chew on the sandwich.

Everyone laughed.

Sammy cried, "That stupid dog," and raced toward him.

Mop ran.

He took off so fast, he yanked the rope out of Sammy's hand.

He darted into a bunch of bushes against the cliff.

Sammy ran after him.

He tried to step on the rope ... but it disappeared after Mop, right into the bushes.

Sammy pushed his way in.

The branches scratched his face and arms.

"Mop! Mop! Here, Mop!" he called. "Where are you, Moppy?"

Mop barked, "Woof! Woof!"

But the sound of barking was coming from way above the bushes.

Mop was up on the cliff!

Everyone ran after Sammy into the bushes.

Behind the bushes they saw an opening in the cliff.

It looked like a skinny stone doorway.

Inside the doorway was a steep stone path.

They climbed up until they were all standing on the cliff.

Sammy grabbed Mop and hugged him. Then he tied Mop's rope to his belt. And right there, right where they stood, was a large cave opening.

They took hold of some bushes and pulled themselves inside. They were standing in a space as big as a living room.

The ceiling formed a huge curve. They looked out at the river valley below.

The wall on the left was covered with reddish-brown drawings.

The floor was covered with loose dirt-like stuff.

Sammy pushed some of it aside with his hands. Then he reached into it until his whole arm was covered.

He said, "Wow! This is all stones and bones. Here's a tiny skull, small as my thumbnail."

Mr. Adams yelled, "YIPEE! YOU DID IT! YOU FOUND IT! IT'S REAL! MY GRANDPA'S CAVE!"

Then he said, "Quick, give me the radio."

He pressed the button.

He said, "Dave! You did it! Mop found an opening in the cliff. We found the cave, right where you thought! We are in it, this minute!

"We can look through the trees and

114

see your balloon.

"It's beautiful here. The cave is beautiful. The Woodlanders are beautiful!"

They looked around at each other. They all were sweaty and dirty, and had twigs sticking out of their clothes and hair.

With that, everyone began to laugh.

It was late that evening.

They were all back at the ranch house, in the dining room.

On the table in front of them lay a map.

Jackie Lee, the chief park ranger, had flown to the ranch by helicopter.

She was saying, "Our team of scientists will sift through everything on the cave floor. Who knows what they'll find out about the people who used the cave!

"The team will study the cave for a year. They'll watch the sun on the cave walls. There's a chance that this cave is a stone calendar."

Jackie leaned over Dave and looked at the map. Mr. Adams and Tyler showed her the exact spot where the cave was.

Mr. Adams pointed to the map. He said, "And here's the doorway that Mop found in the cliff wall."

Jackie said, "I'm in charge of naming these new finds. Since we are all here, Tyler has something to tell you."

Tyler said, "I'm writing in three new names on this map. The first is ADAMS CAVE!"

He wrote in the name.

Everyone clapped.

He went on. "And Jackie has decided to name the cliff below the cave WOODLANDERS CLIFF!"

Mr. Adams and the rangers clapped and cheered.

Jackie said, "And last, we are naming the opening that led up to the cliff. From now on, forever, it will be known as MOP'S DOORWAY."

Mop barked at the sound of his name.

The cheering could have been heard all the way up to the cave.

Mrs. Tandy said, "And now, I have a surprise. We have baked a double batch of oatmeal cookies on the wood-burning stove."

She marched through the kitchen door and brought back a HUGE plate of golden-brown cookies.

Mrs. Adams brought in some milk.

Bill brought glasses.

Sammy took a whole handful of cookies. He said, "These go to Mop, the great detective dog. He always knows when something's fishy!"

He took another handful. "And these go to me, best friend of the great detective dog."

Then, laughing and munching, the Woodlanders and their friends talked late into the night.